Disney · PIXAR

Cars

P9-DUB-838

PEDAL TO THE METAL

A GOLDEN BOOK • NEW YORK

www.randomhouse.com/kids/disney

ISBN: 978-0-7364-2555-1

MANUFACTURED IN MALAYSIA

10 9 8 7 6 5 4 3 2 1

Faster than fast!

Quicker than quick!

He's Lightning McQueen!

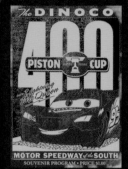

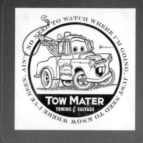

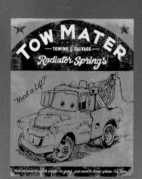

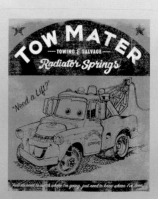

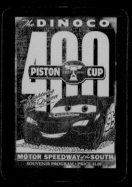

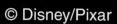

Connect the dots to see McQueen's lucky sticker!

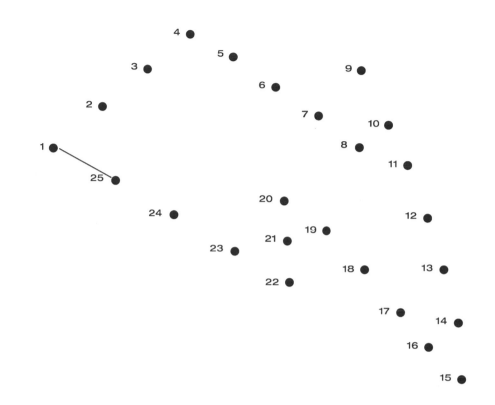

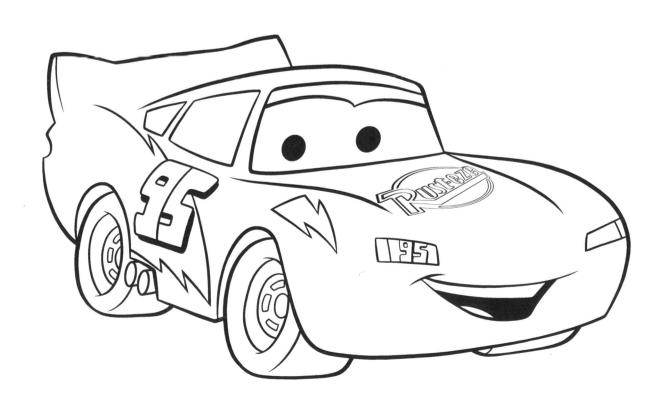

McQueen loves the spotlight.

The King is the world's greatest racing champion.

Chick Hicks thinks he can beat The King!

The race is on!

Pop! McQueen blows a tire!

No time for a pit stop!

Photo finish!

1st TO THE FINISH!

BURNING up the TRACK!

LEAVING THE COMPETITION IN THE DUST

KING VS McQueen 08

Vitoline RACING TEAM

TAKING THE RACE BY STORM!

TAKING THE RACE BY STORM!

Vitoline RACING TEAM

NiTROADE RACING TEAM

Vitoline
RACING TEAM

95
Lightning McQueen

easy IDLE
Racing Team

No Stall

BURNING up the TRACK!

Vitoline
RACING TEAM

Team RETREAD

RE-VOLTING
RACING TEAM

King VS McQueen
08

LEAVING THE COMPETITION IN THE DUST

95
Lightning McQueen

McQueen barely makes it to the finish line!

What does the pit crew call McQueen?
Use the code below to find out!

A	E	H	M	N	O	R	S	W

McQueen meets his sponsors.

Can you find the real McQueen?
(Hint: He's the one that's different!)

A

B

C

D

ANSWER: B.

Off to the big race!

Unscramble the letters below to find out who drives McQueen to all the racetracks.

C M K A

_ _ _ _

ANSWER: Mack.

Wake up, Mack!

Wrong way, McQueen!

© Disney/Pixar

© Disney/Pixar

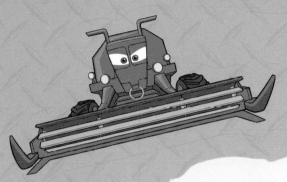

Sheriff is on patrol!

McQueen makes a mess in Radiator Springs!

Take cover!

Find 3 things that are different in the bottom picture.

ANSWER: 1) There is a second cone on the ground; 2) the moon is facing the opposite direction; and 3) the cactus is upside down.

Impounded!

Mater is a tow truck.
How many times can you find the name MATER in the puzzle?
Look up, down, forward, backward, and diagonally.

```
T M A T E R
M R T M R E
A E E A E T
T T A T T A
E A T E A M
R M A R R M
```

Here comes the judge . . . Doc Hudson!

Sally listens as McQueen tells his story.

LIGHTNING McQUEEN

95

FABULOUS HUDSON HORNET

95

OFFROAD MAYHEM!

Ferrari

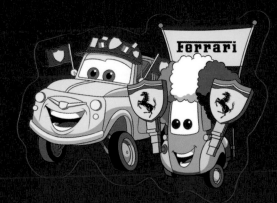

Lightning McQueen

95

95

SHERIFF

Lightning McQueen

95

95

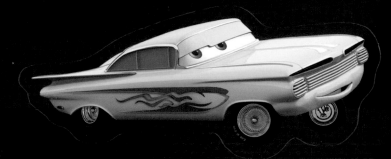

Lightning McQueen

Doc orders McQueen to fix the road.

McQueen must use Bessie to fix the road.
Use the code below to find out what Bessie is.

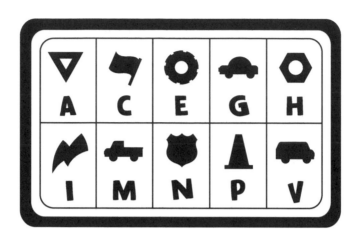

ANSWER: A paving machine.

Sally owns the Cozy Cone Motel.
She offers McQueen a place to stay.

Flo runs the local café.

Can you figure out which is the real Ramone?
(Hint: He's the one that's different!)

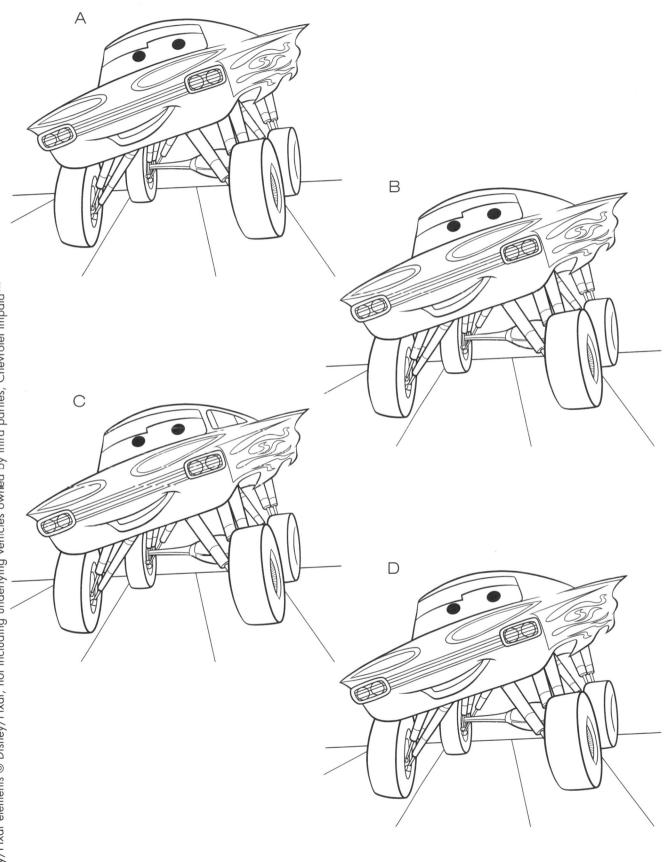

A

B

C

D

ANSWER: C.

Luigi owns the tire shop.

Guido works with Luigi.

Guido loves to change tires!

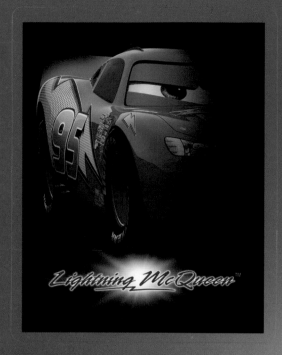

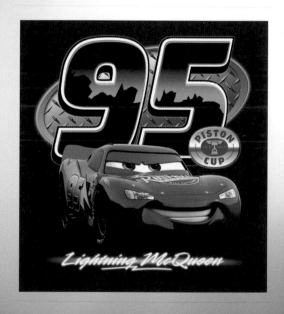

LIGHTNING McQUEEN
SPEED. I AM SPEED.

CHEWALL

MAR CARBURETOR COUNTY 42
41WW2
VETERAN

TOW MATER
TOWING & SALVAGE

SHERIFF

LIGHTNING McQUEEN
SPEED. I AM SPEED.

Disney · PIXAR

Cars

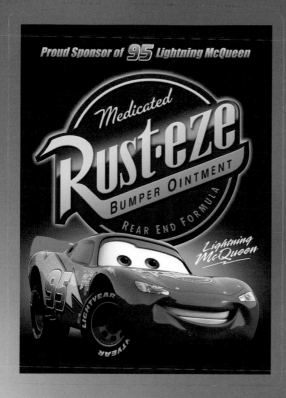

What docs Fillmore make?
Unscramble the word below to find out!

L U E F

__ __ __ __

ANSWER: Fuel.

Sarge owns the supply shop.

Lizzie is the oldest car in Radiator Springs!

Red is a big fire truck. He's shy.

McQueen runs out of gas.

Doc challenges McQueen to a race!

McQueen doesn't know that Doc used to be a famous race car!

McQueen takes the lead!

DINOCO

95

easy IDLE
A Warm Start To A Cold Morning

GASPRIN
HOOD ACHE RELIEF

95

Vitoline
FOR OLDER ACTIVE CARS

Lightning McQueen

Interstate

95

DINOCO

PISTON CUP

LeaK
Less
ADULT DRIP PANS

95

N2O

RE·VOLTING
REBUILT ALTERNATORS

Medicated
Rust·eze
BUMPER OINTMENT
REAR END FORMULA

95

Creme Filled
Gask·its
The Racetrack Treat

 Rust-eze

 OCTANE GAIN
TURBO VITAMINS

 MOTION DOCTOR

 No Stall

95

95

 RETREAD TIRE DEODORANT · ROLL ON

 95

N₂O

 CERTIFIED OIL ORGANIC

 N₂O

MOOD SPRINGS

 Lightning McQueen

 NITROADE HI-ENERGY DRINK

 CLUTCH + AID

 LIL' TORQUEY PISTONS

 95

 N₂O

 95

 RPM
Nighttime Backfire Suppressant

 Medicated Rust-eze BUMPER OINTMENT · REAR END FORMULA

© Disney/Pixar

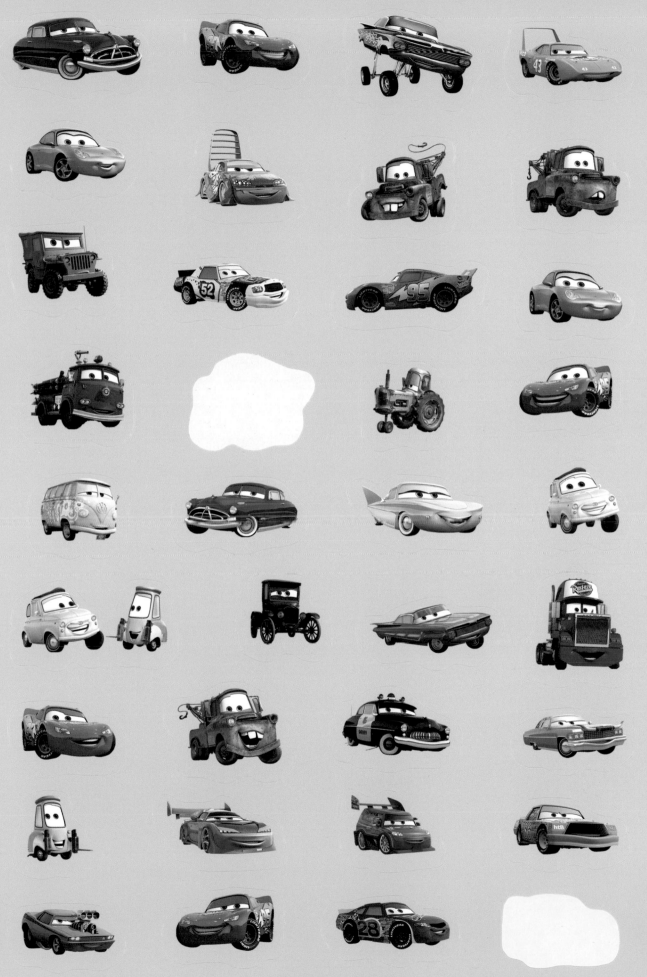

© Disney/Pixar

Watch out!

What does Mater use to pull McQueen out of the ditch?
To find out, begin at the arrow and write each of the letters
in order on the lines below.

© Disney/Pixar

___ ___ ___ ___ ___ ___ ___ ___ ___

McQueen needs new tires.

McQueen finds one of Doc's Piston Cups!

Doc tells McQueen his sad story.

What does McQueen tell everyone that Doc won?
Use the code below to find out!

▽	🚐	🛡	🚗	⭕	⚡	⭕	🚩	🚚	⬡	⯅
C	E H	I	N	O	P	R	S	T	U

Mater and Sally enjoy the new road.

Find 5 things that are different in the bottom picture.

ANSWER: 1) The mountains are facing a different direction; 2) Mater has no tow cable; 3) McQueen has no Rust-eze logo; 4) Mater is missing a headlight; and 5) there is no flag.

© Disney/Pixar

Flo and Ramone like to cruise low and slow.

Everyone in town goes for a drive!

McQueen leaves for the big race.

The race begins! But McQueen misses his friends.

McQueen meets his new pit crew!

Oh, no! Not again!

Pit stop!

Lightning McQueen™

HUDSON
DOCTOR HUDSON
DR. OF INTERNAL COMBUSTION

DOC HUDSON

RADIATOR SPRINGS' VERY OWN *LIVING LEGEND*

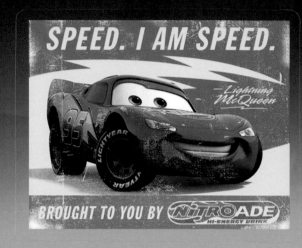

SPEED. I AM SPEED.

Lightning McQueen

BROUGHT TO YOU BY NiTROADE HI-ENERGY DRINK

LIGHTNING McQUEEN

Lightning McQueen

SPEED. I AM SPEED.

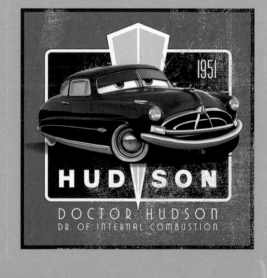

1951

HUDSON
DOCTOR HUDSON
DR. OF INTERNAL COMBUSTION

TOW MATER

TOWING & SALVAGE | Radiator Springs

95
Lightning McQueen

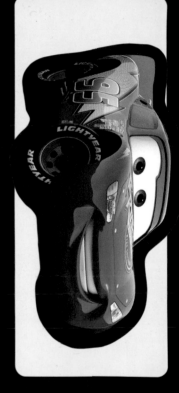

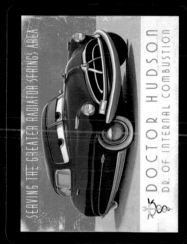

Speedway LEGEND DOC HUDSON

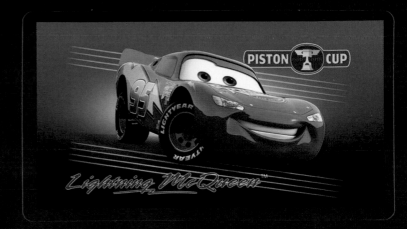

PISTON CUP

Lightning McQueen™

DOC HUDSON

RADIATOR SPRINGS' VERY OWN LIVING LEGEND

AIN'T NO NEED TO WATCH WHERE I'M GOING. JUST NEED TO KNOW WHERE I'VE BEEN.

TOW MATER
TOWING & SALVAGE

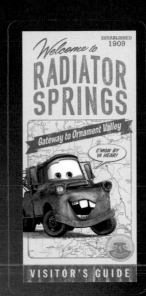

ESTABLISHED
1909

Welcome to
RADIATOR SPRINGS

Gateway to Ornament Valley

C'MON BY YA HEAR!

VISITOR'S GUIDE

PISTON RACING SERIES CUP

The DINOCO 400
CALIFORNIA

SUNDAY MAY 20

THE RACE FOR THE CHAMPIONSHIP ENDS HERE!

RACE PROGRAM

95
Lightning McQueen

RADIATOR SPRINGS

SHERIFF

KEEPER OF THE PEACE

TOW MATER
TOWING & SALVAGE
Radiator Springs

Need a Lift?

The DINOCO 400
A PISTON CUP Championship Series Race

Lightning McQueen™

Rust-eze

95

RPM
Nighttime Backfire Suppressant

TOW MATER
TOWING & SALVAGE

LIL' TORQUEY PISTONS

MAR CARBURETOR COUNTY 42
41WW2
VETERAN

LIGHTYEAR

Chick Hicks bumps The King!

Chick Hicks wins the big race!

McQueen helps a friend!

McQueen returns to his new home—Radiator Springs!